*Railway Series, No. 11*

# PERCY THE SMALL ENGINE

by
## THE REV. W. AWDRY

with illustrations by
C. REGINALD DALBY

**KAYE & WARD LIMITED**

*First published by*
*Edmund Ward (Publishers) Ltd 1956*
*Fourth paperback edition 1984 by Kaye & Ward Ltd*
*The Windmill Press, Kingswood, Tadworth, Surrey*

*Copyright © 1967 Kaye & Ward Ltd*

ISBN 0 7182 1048 4

*Printed and bound in Great Britain by*
*William Clowes Limited, Beccles and London*

DEAR CHRISTOPHER, AND GILES, AND PETER, AND CLIVE,

Thank you for writing to ask for a book about Percy. He is still cheeky, and we were afraid (the Fat Controller and I) that if he had a book to himself, it might make him cheekier than ever, and that would never do!

But Percy has been such a Really Useful Engine that we both think he deserves a book. Here it is.

THE AUTHOR

## Percy and the Signal

PERCY is a little green tank-engine who works in the Yard at the Big Station. He is a funny little engine, and loves playing jokes. These jokes sometimes get him into trouble.

"Peep peep!" he whistled one morning. "Hurry up, Gordon! the train's ready."

Gordon thought he was late and came puffing out.

"Ha ha!" laughed Percy, and showed him a train of dirty coal trucks.

Gordon didn't go back to the shed.

He stayed on a siding thinking how to pay Percy out.

"Stay in the Shed today," squeaked Percy to James. "The Fat Controller will come and see you."

James was a conceited engine. "Ah!" he thought, "the Fat Controller knows I'm a fine engine, ready for anything. He wants me to pull a Special Train."

So James stayed where he was, and nothing his Driver and Fireman could do would make him move.

But the Fat Controller never came, and the other engines grumbled dreadfully.

They had to do James' work as well as their own.

At last an Inspector came. "Show a wheel, James," he said crossly. "You can't stay here all day."

"The Fat Controller told me to stay here," answered James sulkily. "He sent a message this morning."

"He did not," retorted the Inspector. "How could he? He's away for a week."

"Oh!" said James. "Oh!" and he came quickly out of the Shed. "Where's Percy?" Percy had wisely disappeared!

When the Fat Controller came back, he *did* see James, and Percy too. Both engines wished he hadn't!

James and Gordon wanted to pay Percy out; but Percy kept out of their way. One morning, however, he was so excited that he forgot to be careful.

"I say, you engines," he bubbled, "I'm to take some trucks to Thomas' Junction. The Fat Controller chose me specially. He must know I'm a Really Useful Engine."

"More likely he wants you out of the way," grunted James.

But Gordon gave James a wink. . . . Like this.

"Ah yes," said James, "just so. . . . You were saying, Gordon . . . ?"

"James and I were just speaking about signals at the Junction. We can't be too careful about signals. But then, I needn't say that to a Really Useful Engine like you, Percy."

Percy felt flattered.

"Of course not," he said.

"We had spoken of 'backing signals'," put in James. "They need extra special care, you know. Would you like me to explain?"

"No thank you, James," said Percy airily. "I know all about signals," and he bustled off importantly.

James and Gordon solemnly exchanged winks!

Percy was a little worried as he set out.

"I wonder what 'backing signals' are?" he thought.

"Never mind, I'll manage. I know all about signals." He puffed crossly to his trucks, and felt better.

He saw a signal just outside the Station. "Bother!" he said. "It's at 'danger'."

"Oh! Oh! Oh!" screamed the trucks as they bumped into each other.

Presently the signal moved to show "line clear". Its arm moved up instead of down. Percy had never seen that sort of signal before. He was surprised.

" 'Down' means 'go'," he thought, "and 'up' means 'stop', so 'upper still' must mean 'go back'. I know! it's one of those 'backing signals'. How clever of me to find that out."

"Come on, Percy," said his Driver, "off we go."

But Percy wouldn't go forward, and his Driver had to let him "back" in order to start at all.

"I am clever," thought Percy, "even my Driver doesn't know about 'backing signals'," and he started so suddenly that the trucks screamed again.

"Whoah! Percy," called his Driver. "Stop! You're going the wrong way."

"But it's a 'backing signal'," Percy protested, and told him about Gordon and James. The Driver laughed, and explained about signals that point up.

"Oh dear!" said Percy, "let's start quickly before they come and see us."

But he was too late. Gordon swept by with the Express, and saw everything.

The big engines talked about signals that night. They thought the subject was funny. They laughed a lot. Percy thought they were being very silly!

# Duck Takes Charge

"Do you know what?" asked Percy.

"What?" grunted Gordon.

"Do you know what?"

"Silly," said Gordon crossly, "of course I don't know what, if you don't tell me what what is."

"The Fat Controller says that the work in the Yard is too heavy for me. He's getting a bigger engine to help me."

"Rubbish!" put in James. "Any engine could do it," he went on grandly. "If you worked more and chattered less, this Yard would be a sweeter, a better, and a happier place."

Percy went off to fetch some coaches.

"That stupid old signal," he thought, "no one listens to me now. They think I'm a silly little engine, and order me about.

"I'll show them! I'll show them!" he puffed as he ran about the Yard. But he didn't know how.

Things went wrong, the coaches and trucks behaved badly and by the end of the afternoon he felt tired and unhappy.

He brought some coaches to the Station, and stood panting at the end of the platform.

"Hullo Percy!" said the Fat Controller, "you look tired."

"Yes, Sir, I am, Sir; I don't know if I'm standing on my dome or my wheels."

"You look the right way up to me," laughed the Fat Controller. "Cheer up! The new engine is bigger than you, and can probably do the work alone. Would you like to help build my new harbour at Thomas' Junction? Thomas and Toby will help; but I need an engine there all the time."

"Oh yes, Sir, thank you, Sir!" said Percy happily.

The new engine arrived next morning.

"What is your name?" asked the Fat Controller kindly.

"Montague, Sir; but I'm usually called 'Duck'. They say I waddle; I don't really, Sir, but I like 'Duck' better than Montague."

"Good!" said the Fat Controller. " 'Duck' it shall be. Here Percy, come and show 'Duck' round."

The two engines went off together. At first the trucks played tricks, but soon found that playing tricks on Duck was a mistake! The coaches behaved well, though James, Gordon and Henry did not.

They watched Duck quietly doing his work. "He seems a simple sort of engine," they whispered, "we'll have some fun.

"Quaa-aa-aak! Quaa-aa-aak!" they wheezed as they passed him.

Percy was cross; but Duck took no notice. "They'll get tired of it soon," he said.

Presently the three engines began to order Duck about.

Duck stopped. "Do they tell you to do things, Percy?" he asked.

"Yes they do," answered Percy sadly.

"Right," said Duck, "we'll soon stop *that* nonsense." He whispered something. . . . "We'll do it tonight."

The Fat Controller had had a good day. There had been no grumbling passengers, all the trains had run to time, and Duck had worked well in the Yard.

The Fat Controller was looking forward to hot buttered toast for tea at home.

He had just left the office when he heard an extraordinary noise. "Bother!" he said, and hurried to the Yard.

Henry, Gordon and James were Wheeeeeshing and snorting furiously; while Duck and Percy calmly sat on the points outside the Shed, refusing to let the engines in.

"STOP THAT NOISE," he bellowed.

"Now Gordon."

"They won't let us in," hissed the big engine crossly.

"Duck, explain this behaviour."

"Beg pardon, Sir, but I'm a Great Western Engine. We Great Western Engines do our work without Fuss; but we are *not* ordered about by other engines. You, Sir, are our Controller. We will of course move if you order us; but, begging your pardon, Sir, Percy and I would be glad if you would inform these—er— engines that we only take orders from you."

The three big engines hissed angrily.

"SILENCE!" snapped the Fat Controller. "Percy and Duck, I am pleased with your work today; but *not* with your behaviour tonight. You have caused a Disturbance."

Gordon, Henry and James sniggered. They stopped suddenly when the Fat Controller turned on them. "As for you," he thundered, "you've been worse. You made the Disturbance. Duck is quite right. This is My Railway, and I give the orders."

When Percy went away, Duck was left to manage alone.

He did so . . . easily!

## Percy and Harold

PERCY worked hard at the Harbour. Toby helped, but sometimes the loads of stone were too heavy, and Percy had to fetch them for himself. Then he would push the trucks along the quay to where the workmen needed the stone for their building.

An airfield was close by, and Percy heard the aeroplanes zooming overhead all day. The noisiest of all was a helicopter, which hovered, buzzing like an angry bee.

"Stupid thing!" said Percy, "why can't it go and buzz somewhere else?"

One day Percy stopped near the airfield. The helicopter was standing quite close.

"Hullo!" said Percy, "who are you?"

"I'm Harold, who are you?"

"I'm Percy. What whirly great arms you've got."

"They're nice arms," said Harold, offended. "I can hover like a bird. Don't you wish *you* could hover?"

"Certainly not; I like my rails, thank you."

"I think railways are slow," said Harold in a bored voice. "They're not much use, and quite out of date." He whirled his arms and buzzed away.

Percy found Toby at the Top Station arranging trucks.

"I say, Toby," he burst out, "that Harold, that stuck-up whirlibird thing, says I'm slow and out of date. Just let him wait, I'll show him!"

He collected his trucks and started off, still fuming.

Soon above the clatter of the trucks they heard a familiar buzzing.

"Percy," whispered his Driver, "there's Harold. He's not far ahead. Let's race him."

"Yes, let's," said Percy excitedly, and quickly gathering speed, he shot off down the line.

The Guard's wife had given him a flask of tea for "elevenses". He had just poured out a cup when the Van lurched and he spilt it down his uniform. He wiped up the mess with his handkerchief, and staggered to the front platform.

Percy was pounding along, the trucks screamed and swayed, while the Van rolled and pitched like a ship at sea.

"Well, I'll be ding-dong-danged!" said the Guard.

Then he saw Harold buzzing alongside, and understood.

"Go it, Percy!" he yelled. "You're gaining."

Percy had never been allowed to run fast before; he was having the time of his life!

"Hurry! Hurry! Hurry!" he panted to the trucks.

"We-don't-want-to; we-don't-want-to," they grumbled; but it was no use, Percy was bucketing along with flying wheels, and Harold was high and alongside.

The Fireman shovelled for dear life, while the Driver was so excited he could hardly keep still.

"Well done, Percy," he shouted, "we're gaining! We're going ahead! Oh good boy, good boy!"

Far ahead, a "distant signal" warned them that the Wharf was near. Shut off steam, whistle, "Peep, peep, peep, brakes, Guard, please." Using Percy's brakes too, the Driver carefully checked the train's headlong speed. They rolled under the main line, and halted smoothly on the Wharf.

"Oh dear!" groaned Percy, "I'm sure we've lost."

The Fireman scrambled to the cab roof. "We've won! we've won!" he shouted and nearly fell off in his excitement.

"Harold's still hovering. He's looking for a place to land!"

"Listen boys!" the Fireman called. "Here's a song for Percy."

Said Harold helicopter to our Percy, "You are slow!
Your Railway is out of date and not much use, you know."
But Percy, with his stone-trucks, did the trip in record time;
And we beat that helicopter on Our Old Branch Line.*

The Driver and Guard soon caught the tune, and so did the workmen on the quay.

Percy loved it. "Oh thank you!" he said. He liked the last line best of all.

*See page 64 for the music for this song.

# Percy's Promise

A MOB of excited children poured out of Annie and Clarabel one morning, and raced down to the beach.

"They're the Vicar's Sunday School," explained Thomas. "I'm busy this evening, but the Station-master says I can ask you to take them home."

"Of course I will," promised Percy.

The children had a lovely day. But at tea-time it got very hot. Dark clouds loomed overhead. Then came lightning, thunder, and rain. The children only just managed to reach shelter before the deluge began.

Annie and Clarabel stood at the platform.
The children scrambled in.

"Can we go home please, Station-master?"
asked the Vicar.

The Station-master called Percy. "Take the
children home quickly please," he ordered.

The rain streamed down on Percy's boiler.
"Ugh!" he shivered, and thought of his nice
dry shed. Then he remembered.

"A promise is a promise," he told himself,
"so here goes."

His Driver was anxious. The river was rising
fast. It foamed and swirled fiercely, threatening
to flood the country any minute.

The rain beat in Percy's face. "I wish I could see, I wish I could see," he complained.

They left a cutting, and found themselves in water. "Oooh my wheels!" shivered Percy. "It's cold!" but he struggled on.

"Oooooooooooooooshshshshshsh!" he hissed, "it's sloshing my fire."

They stopped and backed the coaches to the cutting and waited while the Guard found a telephone.

He returned looking gloomy.

"We couldn't go back if we wanted," he said, "the bridge near the Junction is down."

The Fireman went to the Guard's Van carrying a hatchet.

"Hullo!" said the Guard, "you look fierce."

"I want some dry wood for Percy's fire, please."

They broke up some boxes, but that did not satisfy the Fireman. "I'll have some of your floor boards," he said.

"What! my nice floor," grumbled the Guard. "I only swept it this morning," but he found a hatchet and helped.

Soon they had plenty of wood stored in Percy's bunker. His fire burnt well now. He felt warm and comfortable again.

"Buzzzzzzzzzzzzzzzz! Buzzzzzzzzzzzzzzzz! Buzzzzzzzzzzzzzzzz!"

"Oh dear!" thought Percy sadly, "Harold's come to laugh at me."

Bump! Something thudded on Percy's boiler. "Ow!" he exclaimed in a muffled voice, "that's really too bad! He needn't *throw* things."

His driver unwound a parachute from Percy's indignant front.

"Harold isn't throwing things at you," he laughed, "he's dropping hot drinks for us."

They all had a drink of cocoa, and felt better.

Percy had steam up now. "Peep peep! Thank you, Harold!" he whistled. "Come on, let's go."

The water lapped his wheels. "Ugh!" he shivered. It crept up and up and up. It reached his ash-pan, then it sloshed at his fire. "Oooooooooooooooshshshshshshshshshshshshsh!"

Percy was losing steam; but he plunged bravely on. "I promised," he panted, "I promised."

They piled his fire high with wood, and managed to keep him steaming.

"I *must* do it," he gasped, "I must, I must, I must."

He made a last great effort, and stood, exhausted but triumphant, on rails which were clear of the flood.

He rested to get steam back, then brought the train home.

"Three cheers for Percy!" called the Vicar, and the children nearly raised the roof!

The Fat Controller arrived in Harold. First he thanked the men. "Harold told me you were—er—wizard, Percy. He says he can beat you at some things . . ."

Percy snorted.

" . . . but *not* at being a submarine." He chuckled. "I don't know what you've both been playing at, and I won't ask! But I do know that you're a Really Useful Engine."

"Oh Sir!" whispered Percy happily.

Tune by W. AWDRY

Notation by E. TRUNDLE

Said Har - old hel - i - cop - ter to our Per - cy; you are slow;    Your

Rail - way is    out   of date and not much   use you    know!    But

Per - cy with his stone-trucks did  the   trip  in rec - ord  time, And we

beat  that hel - i - cop - ter  on  our  old  Branch  Line